"The Choices We Make"
By: Daryl A. Young

This is a work of fiction. Similarities to real people, places, or events are entirely coincidental.

THE CHOICES WE MAKE

First edition. April 11, 2023.

Copyright © 2023 Daryl Young.

ISBN: 979-8215808238

Written by Daryl Young.

Table of Contents

Chapter 1: 1988

I can recall it like it was yesterday. Mom and dad packed all their belongings along with their three children and headed south to Virginia. Dad had just got a new job at the Nabisco factory five minutes east of Richmond. There he would be the overnight general manager, overseeing the production of the night crew. This position pays three times more than his current position as a call center supervisor for the local cable company in Philadelphia. It's June, summer just begun, my little brother Diageo turned 6 on the first of the month. My oldest Sister Bella-Rae, sixteen years of age, wasn't too thrilled to leave behind her cool friends and the one guy she fancied and dated for 2 years. Bella-Rae was gorgeous, all the guys in the neighborhood, from my block to my best friend's block 3 miles west wanted her. She always played hard to get or played some game on the young teenage guys. Getting them to buy her whatever she wanted one day and the next, leaving them high and dry. Not even speaking to them or acknowledging their presence. She did that to a lot of them and some multiple times. Who would blame her though? Fool me once, shame on you. Fool me twice, shame on me. Bella is 5'6 dark brown, long wavy hair to the middle of her back, pristine white teeth, curvy and busty for a teenager. Let's just say she never looked her age once she hit puberty. At the age 11 she blossomed, so at sixteen she looked like a twenty-one-year-old college woman and conducted herself as so. Then there is me Nia-Renee; thirteen, shy, brace face, almond brown, short hair to my neck and skinny like a twig. I have just finished junior high and will be turning fourteen next month and will be getting my braces removed finally after having them for a little over 3 years. Yeah, my teeth were jacked up! I had a horrific crossbite. My teeth never lined up prior to me getting my braces, so I was excited I was near the end of the journey of me fixing my smile. For the last three months I've prayed to God every night; wishing that for my birthday coming that I at least grow a butt or a B cup. I was tired of living in my sister's shadow. All the guys were stunned by her beauty, even the ones in my grade or lower. As the seasons change, so do our lives, I've never been a fan of change, but I welcomed this move to Virginia with open arms. I wanted a new scene, where no one knows me, and I can no longer be so shy, and I can create an alter ego. A girl who was vibrant, popular amongst the guys and girls just like Bella. Unbeknown to me God was listening and heard my prayers because soon everything I wanted now will soon come into fruition and be my reality.

My mom Cynthia is 37, short woman standing only 4'11 light brown, short brown curly hair that looked red in the summertime. She was born and raised in Philly in 1951, the best time to be born if you let her tell it. My father Andre, 38 and originally from Charleston, SC was a very tall dark handsome fella. He's 6'3 with a low-cut with the sides and back faded, waves on top, a goatee, very athletic and such a snazzy dresser. My parents met at Virginia State University (VSU), an HBCU (Historically Black College or University), located 20 minutes south of Richmond. My mom was a Woo Woo, the name given to VSU cheerleaders, and she was a damn good one at that. She was the captain of the squad in her junior and senior years. My father was an MVP basketball star for the University, for the whole time he was there. Dad will always tell the story of how mom and he met just about every time he gets. He was so proud to be her husband and she was proud to be his wife. It was the fall of 1969 during homecoming when they were introduced by their mutual friend John, who my siblings and I call Uncle John. Dad would always say Mom was cheering for him whenever he was out on the court. He said she would make so much noise whenever he makes a basket, he knew she had to be his. Mom on the other hand brags differ. She says dad followed her all-around campus and even took a course that wasn't required for his major, just to be with her. How flattering, right? Mother was intrigued by his interest in her. Nonetheless they graduated in the spring of 1973 then came back to my mother's hometown Philadelphia and worked. Dad of course majored in business but no company at that time would dare hire a black man as a manager or even run their company. So, he had to settle to get the bills paid plus my parents had already given birth to Bella in the spring before, in '72. Mom of course was a Registered Nurse, that was the job for many women during that decade and the decades before besides being a housekeeper. They managed to save enough money to buy a home. Which was purchased in February of 1975 because my parents were already 4 months pregnant with their second but most talented (if you are asking me) child. It was a 3-bedroom 1 bath home with a small kitchen and living room. Not much yard for the kids to run around and play but we made do of what we had. We loved our small home and so did my parents, it was the first piece of land they'd ever purchased. But the time has come for us to move on with my little brother Diageo being born in 1983 I had to then began sharing rooms with Bella. So, this move to Virginia was well needed and deserved. I wanted my own room, duh! Who wants to share a room with their siblings, especially an older one who is much more beautiful than you?

We hit the road, traveling south down to Maryland then Washington, D.C. and finally Virginia. I Knew we was in Virginia or in the south, when I no longer could smell the factories, nasty emissions entering the atmosphere, polluting the fresh air for miles. However, in the south, well Virginia, I can smell tobacco for miles. But this was a more pleasant smell, and I would watch all the farm animals and count sheep as we drive along I95. Viewing the beautiful mountains, hill tops and wonderful open green pastures, big, tall cornfields for miles. Then we enter Richmond, then the downtown section of Richmond which is very historical but so beautiful and full of life. There are stores, all different shops, and restaurants just about every few blocks so there's plenty of places to shop and eat. My parents are aware of the once thriving black community dub the Black Wall Street, Jackson Ward. As we pass by, dad gives the history lessons on all the famous black people that once lived in the area Maggie L. Walker, Bill Bojangles Robinson, and John Mitchell Jr, just to name a few. He educated us on their influence on the people in the area during the time they lived. "Maggie is the first African American woman to charter a bank and hold position as the president." "John Mitchell Jr. the first African American to run his own newspaper company called the Black Planet." "Oh, yeah I can't forget about Bill Bojangles Robinson African American tap dancer, actor, singer and highest paid Black American of his time." Dad also mentioned that he will take us to the museums in Richmond including the Valentine's Museum which houses all of Richmond's history, the good and bad. Now we travel east of Richmond into Varina, which is the far eastern part of Henrico, a suburban county. Nothing but trees and large open fields, most of the land here was underdeveloped. We lived in the Orange Oak suburban community, which consisted of 300 cookie cutter styled homes arranged in different sizes and colors. Our home is so big and elegant, we had a huge yard my dad had purchased 2 acres, we had plenty of land. The home was recently constructed just 20 years prior to us taking ownership. It has 4 bedrooms, 2 full bathrooms, a half bathroom, large kitchen, a nice size living room and dining room, an unfinished basement and attic. Yes, we had so much space, 1,900 square feet and only paid $5,000 more than our original home which was only 1,050 square feet and sat on .45 an acre of land. You get so much more for your money in the south, the north is just a rip-off if you ask me. The house was Blue and White a combination of both my parent's favorite colors and a modern style. The house was renovated 3 years prior; we had moved on up to the eastside just like "The Jefferson's".

That night once we were settled in my mom made a bigger dinner than ever before. She would always cook a big meal when she was happy or extra excited. We ate pork roast, baked mac & cheese, yams, collard greens and corn bread. Mom's cornbread was so sweet and soft it tasted like cake. We all went to bed full, overstuffed to be exact and grateful. Momma hadn't cooked like this in months because she was always working, so she showed off that night. For dessert, momma's world-famous peach cobbler (even though the world hasn't tried it). Golden brown crest with orange caramelized peach filling oozing through pockets on top of the pie. To sweeten the deal, we added French vanilla ice cream on top, wow, so yummy to my tummy, as I recall. "I'll clear the table and clean the dishes tonight" yells out momma. Normally Bella and I would do this every night after dinner, it's part of our chores. I would always clear the table and dry the dishes. Bella's job is to wash the dishes while she colorfully sings, it was our routine. "Yes!" I screamed out of excitement because my belly was full and all I wanted to do is go watch some tv before bedtime. Showtime at the Apollo was on that night, it was the family's favorite show to watch together. I remember we would act out scenes. Daddy and momma both would host together, while the children be the talent. Dancing and singing, we put on a magnificent show making our parents laugh and so proud of our imaginations. "Nia!" "It's on, come on you're going to miss the first act!" Shouts Bella. We danced and sang the whole show. Didn't pay much attention to the talent that was performing on tv, didn't know their names or where they were from. Just knew the songs they sang and placed us on stage in their place. You see it was Bella's and I ultimate dream, to head to the Big Apple aka New York City and be amongst the most affluent socialites. I consider myself to be a creative genius. When I'm not studying or playing around with my little brother Diageo. When I'm not following behind Bella-Rae, bugging her with all my silly questions or trying to be like her. I love to write poems, short stories and sometimes even songs. I love to write, I always told myself, if I'm not onstage performing my own songs I've written, then I will be a writer for the "New York Post", "New York

Times", "The New Yorker" or whoever would hire me. I had dreams and goals, and I would do anything to achieve them.

"Star"

A star I will be!
I proclaimed that since I was just three,
Standing two feet tall,
With barrettes big, beautiful, and small.
I was destined to be great,
Even when I was just eight.
I can feel the success,
Goddamn it! I want to be amongst the best!
I jot my plans on my bedroom walls,
Knowing papa and mama will soon erase it all.
But that didn't stop me from dreaming,
Can't tell me anything.
Just let me be, after all!!

CHAPTER 2: Birthday

I woke up early the morning of July 12, 1988, I was up ready and dressed at 6am. The sun was up as well in full effect; to be honest I don't know who got up first, the sun or me. As I finished up in the bathroom, preparing to run into my parents' bedroom and scream and shout to wake them up, mama and daddy were already out of the bed and in the kitchen. I can smell the aroma of fried apples, bacon, and homemade biscuits in the air. I run down the stairs and before I can hit the kitchen door, daddy shouts and begun to sing "happy birthday to ya, happy birthday to ya, happy birthday!" That's Stevie Wonders song for those who don't know. Overwhelmed with joy, I wear a huge smile, draped from ear to ear, showing all my teeth covered with braces of course. Mama joins in singing, then she begun to set the table as dad runs out of the kitchen and upstairs to wake up Bella and Diageo. "Mama I'm almost a woman now! Only four more years and I'll be on my own and out of your hair." I shouted. "Oh, hush up, you wouldn't know what to do if you were eighteen today." "You'll will still need your father and I help throughout your college years." "So as long as were paying for anything you will follow by our rules." Says mama, while laughing. "These kids are so quick to grow up these days!" "Mama?" "You made waffles too?" I yelled. So excited to see fluffy Belgium waffles sitting to the side on a platter. Mama made the best waffles in the whole world. Better than the Belgium's in my opinion. "You know I did baby; you know I have to make your favorite on your day." "Thank you, mama!" As I ran to her and hugged her tight. "Of course, sweetheart!" Shortly after, Dad, Diageo and Bella enter the room all with gifts in hand. "Happy birthday Nia!" Yells my little brother Diageo. "Happy Birthday five head!" "Your chest is starting to grow, now you don't have to stuff your bra!" says Bella, laughingly. I didn't even notice myself until it was brought to my attention. So, if my chest is growing, I wonder what my behind is doing. I jumped out of my chair and ran to Bella's room, where she has a long mirror in her room. Big enough for a full body view. Standing there in the mirror admiring my new body that just only started transforming. "I hope my butt grow bigger than Bella's, please, please, please." I shout out with my hands together as if I'm saying a real prayer. Now I know for sure when the school year starts in September, that my milkshake will bring all the boys to the yard. Even though my parents always told me true beauty comes from within. It's not all about how you look but how intelligent and kind you are. Mama and Daddy didn't know how this generation worked. You have got to have a nice figure, a complimenting body to go with that great personality and let's not forget a pretty smile as well. See America will do that to you, with all the beautiful people you see on tv and in the magazines. Their lavish lifestyles, with all the latest brands, cool parties, and day hobbies. I too wanted to be amid it all. I want all the attention from both men and women, I want to drink mimosa's during the day while being interviewed by some fabulous magazine or news show. I want to drink wine during the evening and cocktails at night, while sitting, talking to the host of the late-night show (I've mentioned alcohol a few times purposefully, it's what the superstars drink). Be able to turn down jobs only because I can do so. Yes, the joy of being your own boss and calling all the shots. I have big dreams to write, produce, direct and maybe star in my own show. Bring it all into fruition; I am very ambitious and would do whatever to make it happen. For now, I'll hold my dreams close, keeping them between my family and God (leaving out the parts my parents wouldn't approve of) in hopes of manifesting them to life. I returned downstairs to eat my birthday breakfast and opened my gifts. I was elated for I've received everything I wanted. Makeup thanks to Bella-Rae, a new beautiful purple pencil skirt and a white low-cut blouse from my mom. New shoes and a few journals from dad and little brother. I thanked them all repeatedly, you would've thought I was a child at Disney land.

Later that day my mom took both of her girls out to get our hair and nails done. It was my birthday so I could get a pedicure too, and I did. French tip manicure and pedicure for a sophisticated young lady I am to be. We later met up with dad and Diageo and headed to the movie theater to catch the latest film. For dinner we went to a Hibachi grill, where they cook the food in front of you on a very hot grill. There they performed while cooking our meal, doing tricks with the cooking utensils, and later singing happy birthday to me while holding an ice cream cake with fourteen candles that I blow out. That night ended with my family and I sitting around singing and performing like we always do. The next day, when I got up out of bed, before I could even brush my teeth or comb my hair, I could hear a truck backing up on my street. Beep, beep, beep! I looked out the window and to my surprise a new family was moving into the house directly across from mine. A Puerto Rican family with four kids, two daughters and two sons, mom, dad, and a grandma. "Nia, Bella, Diageo come on, get up! Time to get dressed and go meet and greet our new neighbors moving in." Screams Mama. Father just arrived home from doing a 12-hour overnight shift. In comes dad, he takes his hat off and shoes off at the door and shouts out, "honey I'm home!" "There's a new family moving in directly across the street, have you notice?" Mama replies, "yes, dear and I've prepared a upside down pineapple cake for them." "It's still warm, I hope they like pineapple." As she reaches into dad for a hug and kiss. "How was your shift baby?" "Oh, you know, just another day on the ship. Making sure my boss doesn't have any reason to question my work by keeping production up." "I smell like Oreos, don't I honey?" "You know you do. I can just eat you up with a glass of cold milk." "I love my chocolate; I got a sweet tooth and its aching for you!" Says mama, while rubbing dad's broad shoulders and strong arms. Dad caressing mama's lower back and behind, kissing her all over her face and neck. "Don't you start something you can't finish this morning; the kids are getting ready so we can take this cake over and introduce ourselves first." "Next, I must take Nia to the orthodontist to have her braces removed. Lastly, I'll take care of you sir." Whispered in his ear in a seductive way then kissed him on his cheek. "Okay, we'll see who will be taking care of who later today." Says Dad.

Into the kitchen all three of us walked in. "Morning mama & dad!" Yells all children. "Mama? I thought you were making pancakes. It smells so wonderful!" Shouts Bella. "No baby, it's the cake for the new neighbors that you smell." "You all will have cereal this morning." Said mama while smiling graciously. "I want Cap'N Crunch!" Yells Diageo. "Yes, little man. I'll fix your bowl for you." Says dad while preparing Diageo's breakfast. The girls then prepare their own breakfast. "I'm going to go hop in the shower, get dressed, come down eat breakfast and then I'll be ready to greet the wonderful neighbors baby." "Alright, we will be here waiting for you commander in chief." Says mama. Father then runs out of the kitchen and up the stairs to prepare for his day of introducing the family. Twenty minutes later dad comes down and shouts "I'm ready, come on let's get this started, let me show you all how a southern gentleman like me show hospitality." Out the door walked father than mother and the children tagging along behind. We crossed over the road, walked up the sidewalk leading to the big brick tri-level home painted gray, with white shutters and trim, large porch that wrapped around the house. My father knocked on the neighbors big beautiful red door using the huge lion knocker, he didn't want to use the doorbell. The door swung open and there stood Mr. Rodriguez, tall, standing about 6ft. but not as tall as my father who is 6'3. Mr. Rodriguez had hazel eyes, thin mustache, a chisel chin, brown skin wearing a colorful silk-like shirt with the first four buttons undone. Some khaki shorts, long socks with some flip flops. "Hola, how can I help you?" My father responds, "Hello, we're the East's your neighbors from across the street. My wife and children would like to welcome you and your family to the neighborhood." "I'm Andre, this is my wife beautiful wife Cynthia and our three children Bella-Rae, Nia-Renee, and my little man Diageo. My wife baked y'all a scrumptious upside-down pineapple cake, careful it's still a bit warm, fresh out the oven." As my mom leaned into hand Mr. Rodrigues the cake. "Thank you so much Mr. Andre, allow me to sit this down and grab my family to introduce to yours." "My love, come quickly! Bring the children." As they walk towards the door and all step out onto the porch, Mr. Rodriguez introduces his family. I'm Ruiz by the way, this is my lovely wife of 17 years Marisol, my mother Maria. Our amazing children Isabel, who is 6, Lucia, 16, Mateo, 14, and Santiago who is 8. "What a beautiful family you have here Ruiz." "Where did y'all move here from?" Asks my father while my family and I begin to converse and mingle with the Rodriquez's. "We're from the Bronx, New York." "My wife and I got a great offer to work here. My wife is an ER nurse, soon to be working in the triage unit at the local hospital in Richmond, the Medical College of Virginia (MCV)." "I myself am an Electrician for Virginia Power." We all continued to chat for a little while but then we headed on our way leaving Rodriguez's to finish unpacking and I had an appointment to get to.

On our way to the orthodontist office in Richmond, we rode along the streets close to the riverbank. Through the Shockoe Bottom district then hitting downtown Richmond to Dr. Smiths' office. Once we arrived, his office greeted us as we signed in. "Right this way, you all are going to be in room 3. The doctor will be in soon to look and then we can begin to remove your braces." As we waited for the doctor to step into the room, I pulled my polaroid out and snapped a picture of myself. I pulled a sharpie out of my purse and wrote on the following on the picture. "My last day of being brace face 7-13-88", I then placed it in my purse and began to snap more pics of mom waiting reading Ebony Magazine. She then picked up the Richmond Times Dispatch and saw that the local furniture store is having a sale for the upcoming weekend. "Isn't this an elegant bar set?" "I bet this would look nice in the basement, I think your dad is going to do something to the basement. Make it his own, where he could escape, I guess to Utopia." She began to chuckle at herself. Soon the doctor entered the room, examined my smile, and soon removed the rubber bands, wires, and glue from my mouth. I was stunned by my new smile. Such a pretty smile, teeth whiter than fresh white paint. Of course, I had to capture this moment as well. Snap! Caption: "New Smile, New Me!"

"Bird"

If I was a bird,

I would fly high,

beyond the sky,

let my wings take me,

far away,

to a place where I can be free,

free to be me!

Chapter 3: Autumn & Winter '88

It's the first day of school, the alarm went off around 6am. I jumped out of bed to try to beat Bella-Rae to the bathroom, but she was already up and starting her morning. Bella is a junior in school, that's the eleventh grade. I'm a freshman and was not accustomed to getting up this early unless I wanted to. Don't get me wrong, I was excited about my new chapter in life. New school, new look and soon I will make new friends besides the kids who lived in my neighborhood. "Bella! Don't take all day please I have to shower and do my hair!" "By the way can you unwrap my hair for me?" Bella swings open the bathroom door. "When I'm done getting myself together, you know it takes time to look great, you can't rush beauty, I want to look my best." Over the summer Bella had started playing in makeup, so it became a part of her daily routine, not wanting to leave the house without. Hell, not even answering the door without her face beating and decent hair. My sister was gorgeous, when we went out to the park or supermarket, the folks always thought of her as a model. The full bathroom was in my parents' room, it was theirs and theirs only, all the children understood that. I ran down the stairs to the half bathroom halfway before you hit the kitchen to at least brush my teeth and wash my face. The school bus will arrive soon, so I began to eat breakfast. Shortly after, Bella exits the rest room; with a mouthful of food, I run back up the stairs to shower and finish getting ready. On our way out the door and to the bus stop, we meet up with Rodriguez's kids Lucia and Mateo, who are the same age as us. "Lucia! Hey girl!" Hey Bella, I like that lip gloss it's shimmery and shiny." "Here, you want some?" Bella reaches into her designer purse and pulls out the gloss and hands it to Lucia. "Hey, Nia!" Yells Mateo. "How are you this morning?" Nia replies not so excitedly and a little annoyed. "Hey Mateo, I'm ok just kind of nervous for the first day." Mateo hasn't hit puberty yet, so he still looks twelve. The only thing that has changed is his height. He has grown but not yet tall enough for Nia. No mustache, no muscles and his voice had begun to break. So, Nia didn't pay Mateo any mind not for at least two more years from now. That's when he will be attractive to her eyes. The bus arrived; they all got on along with the other neighborhood kids. Along the way Nia her the older girls chatting in the back with the older boys. Giggling and laughing at every joke. Even harder at the not so funny jokes. By lunch time, I was hungry. There's a McDonalds at the corner before the school. All the juniors and seniors had permission to leave the campus during lunch hour to grab some food of their choice. Mateo and I plotted to sneak off with the other kids, coincidentally, Bella, Lucia, Mateo, and I all had the same lunch period. This became almost a daily thing, we'd run off to McDonald's, grab some food and eat it walking back. High schools were completely different than any other grade school. We had much more freedom, even if we weren't sure what was permitted, like going to the courtyard just to hang out. Most of the students hung out in the courtyard chatting with others. The whole purpose of the courtyard was to study outside of the classroom walls.

Homecoming arrived, for the whole week we did something different to show school spirit that fall. Monday was mix-match day, the students dressed crazy and bizarre not caring what they looked like. Tuesday is an old school day. I dressed like the people did in the 60's or early 70's with my big afro and parachute pants. Wednesday is pajama day, and we all were happy to be in our sleeping clothes that day. Thursday is garden day, if you wanted to plant a flower in the school garden you can or you can just assist others with upkeeping for that day. Friday is pride day we were to wear only the school colors for that day. Orange and black with a little bit of white; our mascot is the tiger.

That Friday we spent most of the time preparing for the football game that night. Prep rallies throughout the day, decorating the stands with balloons and putting confetti shooters near the end of each stand. The school band played a few tunes as the cheerleaders danced and cheered all day. The game was free for all students, but parents and outsiders had to pay. This was our way of making money for the school alongside the bake sales we had every Friday. With the money the school would have a big party at the end of every school year. Our football team was the best in the state, we won all the championships that we made it to. Lake Brita High School was the best at all sports, basketball, football, cheerleading, soccer, lacrosse, tennis and even track and field. I was proud to be a tiger, loved my school, we're a family composed of talented students, brilliant teachers plus an outstanding staff.

It was soon December, two weeks before Christmas, all throughout the school were Christmas decorations. No hall or locker was left uncovered, the joy of Christmas was all in the air. In the lobby stood a 12-foot tree, filled with a onement from everyone that worked or attended the school. We did secret Santa for the entire school, so you may get someone you don't even know. That was fun to me receiving a gift from a stranger, not knowing what they have gotten you. It was the mystery that kept me feeling good throughout the season of giving. Plus, by this time I made quite a few friends, so more giving and more to come for me. For lunch on the last day before winter break, the school prepared a wonderful feast. Ham, turkey, stuffing, string beans, mashed potatoes and gravy, cranberry sauce, soft rolls, and eggnog to wash it all down. Dessert, Christmas cookies, sugar, and gingerbread; I took a few extra to eat during my last two classes. I watched the clock during my last class of the day, wanting to hurry up and get home because mama and papa are taking us out shopping today. The bell rings to let us know the school day has come to an end, I grab my backpack and dash out of the classroom door. "Bye Mrs. Stern, see you next year!" I shouted out not looking back. "Make sure you all complete the packet I've given you all during class. It's not mandatory but if completed you will get extra credit!" squealed Mrs. Stern, as all the children ran out of the class with glee.

That evening upon arriving at home, I could smell fresh baked goods throughout the air. Mama's preparing for a Christmas party that she always had each year. Not forgetting her parents will be joining us this year. It will be my first time visiting there since we moved south. My fathers' parents will be her too without a doubt. Unknown to us, daddy in his spare time has been completing the basement, putting up a ceiling, walls, and carpeted floors. He had also added an extra bathroom, equipped with a shower, sink and toilet so the elderly wouldn't have to come up for much. Father and mother both were the only child, they had no siblings so they enjoyed spoiling their parents whenever they can. "Honey! Kids, come down I have a surprise for you all." We all ran down to the basement, Diageo the first he's fast plus filled with a lot of energy to burn. "How do y'all like it?" asked Dad. "Wow!" We all are amazed at the transformation that has taken place. In addition to the bathroom, he constructed two bedrooms and a living room; all furnished a decorated by him. At this point I think my dad is amazing and can do just about whatever he puts his mind to. He always finishes whatever he starts and has a humorous, loving personality to go along.

My paternal grandparents arrived first, grandpa Stu and Grandma Betty. They drove up from Charleston, South Carolina in their own car. Then five minutes later a cab arrives carrying grandpa & grandma, John and Louella Brown, my mother's parents. Upon their arrival we show them around the house and finally the basement where they would be sleeping for the next three weeks. After helping them unpack, the whole family decides to head out to Richmond for dinner and shopping. Instead of riding along the riverbank until we can't anymore, father decides to take East Broad Street to Miller & Rhodes department store. It sits on E. Broad St. between 5th and 6th Street; this is where we would sit, eat, and then shop. The department store was huge and had 7 floors, a ballroom and three different restaurants to choose from. We decided on the Steak House, it has a great view. It's closer to where Santa was taking photos with all the guests, near the grand Christmas tree adorn with all sorts of ornaments of all shapes and sizes. Shortly after eating a good meal, we took photos with Santa Mrs. Clause, then shopped like it never. We all had money thanks to my parents working hard; they both received bonuses that allowed them to spend more than before.

Christmas morning was full of bliss and joy, we opened presents, sang, danced, and ate food in the shape of snowflakes, reindeer, and Christmas trees. Later we invited Rodriguez's family over to enjoy the festivities. The two families emerged eating, playing games and sharing cultural traditions. It soon began to snow at nightfall, we all went out to play in the snow, apart from the grandparents of course. They stayed inside and made hot cocoa with marshmallows for us to stay warm and enjoy. This year seemed great! What an awesome way to end the year, family, and friends happy all on accord.

"HOPE"
I hope,
I prey,
I dream,
I lay,
I sway,
But over all
I believe there is,
always another way!

Chapter 4: 2017

On the morning of February 8, just right when the sun has started to rise, I've begun to wake. The cold wintery air crept in slowly as the wood in the fireplace burned out; I never really liked the heat from the furnace. I'm a successful journalist for the local news station in Arlington, VA, where I've been for the last 21 years. Today appeared to be one of those days when my secrets of the past start to surface in my mind and body. Knowing what I did back in 1992 and not telling a sole, not even my best friend Sarah. For this secret to stay a secret I had to keep it to myself, not tell a single person. I lay in the bed not moving, wrapped underneath the comforter like a fetus, swaddled. I wonder what his life is like now and if his childhood upbringing was one that anyone would want to have. Nia felt bad about what happened but overall ashamed of her past that keeps on haunting her. The phone rings, it's Sarah. "Hello?" "Heyyyy, girl!" "Hey." Says Nia in an unsatisfying way. "Don't tell me your still in bed!" Shouts Sarah, through the phone loudly with a burst of energy. "No, well kind of." "It's still early, I want to lay for a couple of more hours." "Hell no! We got an appointment at the salon today and I'm not missing it for no one not even you!" "Girl, I look like Frankenstein this morning." Ha, Ha, Ha! They both laughed. "I had some company last night." Says Sarah. "Was it George?" "Yes." says Sarah underneath her breath. George is Sarah on again, off again boyfriend. "I needed it, plus he apologized. You know I can't say no to a good time or those big brown pop eyes of his." "I can write a column or a book about you two and that unstable relationship." "I'm getting up, give me an hour to get ready." "Okay, I'll see you soon." Nia takes a deep breath and exhales. "Sighs!" She then rolls out of bed and into the bathroom and takes a nice warm shower. She swallows her feelings once again, burying them deep inside her hoping they won't resurface.

Shortly after, Sarah arrives and knocks on the door. Nia opens the door. "You ready?" "Yeah, let me grab my coat and purse." Along the way they go through a drive-thru at a fast-food restaurant for breakfast. Blasting Beyonce Formation, singing and dancing in the car. At the beauty salon they both got a wash plus a blowout, dyed with pin curls. Nia had started feeling much better as the day progressed, as her and Sarah continued their day out and about. Sarah had to stop to get some gas. "I can go pay for the gas but you're pumping." Says Nia. "Cool, grab some flaming hots, please!" Nia puts her thumb up to signal, that she will. While in the store shopping, she bumps into a fine gentleman who goes by the name of Terrance. "Oh, excuse me, I'm sorry!" "I should be more careful." "No, not an issue. How are you, I'm Terrance by the way but My friends call me Tee." Standing there looking up into his eyes, admiring his broad shoulders and his handsome look. Terrance is 6'1, light brown, bald head with a beard and mustache connected to his sideburns, full pink lips, and pearly white teeth. Talk about a snack, he's a meal! "I'm doing wonderful, thanks for asking." "You're welcome, are you from Arlington?" "No, I'm originally from Varina. Well Philadelphia actually, but I've been in Virginia since I was fourteen, and decided to settle in the northern neck of VA after college." "I went to school in DC, Howard University." "HU!" "You know!" Says Nia laughingly. "Sweet, I'm from Richmond, the south side area, born and raised. I graduated from the other HU, Hampton University." "I'm only here visiting my frat brothers for the weekend." "I pledged Alpha Phi Alpha." "Nice!" "I didn't pledge I couldn't find the time, I was too into my studies, I doubled majored." "Really, I like that, a dedicated smart woman." "Wait you look kind of familiar but I'm not sure where I've seen you before." Nia smiles, but not saying you probably seen me on the local news. "Yeah, I get that a lot." "May I give you my contact info if that's ok with you?" "I think you're beautiful, stunning actually!" "My frat brothers and I are having a party later on tonight and would like for you and your friends, if possible, to come by." "Sure!" Says Nia, while handing Terrance her phone. Tee than puts his number in her phone, save it under New Bae Tee and hands her back the phone. "See you soon!" He says smiling while walking away to the register to check out then exit the store. Shortly Nia exits the store and runs to Sarah to tell her all about the guy she just met. "Did you see that fine brother exits the store?" "No, I was taking a selfie to post on my Instagram." "I'm feeling this new color and due." While snapping more pics. Sarah then pumps the gas and soon pulls away. In the car Nia explains her run in with the handsome gentleman and let Sarah know that they've been invited to a party later tonight. "Party!" "You know I'm game, I love to have a good time and meet new people." "Plus, it's a frat party it's going to be men everywhere!" "Hopefully, you'll find a new man so you can stop dealing with George lying ass!" "Ha, ha, ha! Yeah, that idiot is a lying son of a gun." "But he got great sex, what a bad combination."

Later that night while at Sarah's condo, Nia contacts Tee, after searching for his number and realizing what name he saved it under. She blushes and laughs out loud the whole 20 minutes she is on the phone with him. "So, are you and your ladies coming to the party tonight?" "I can send you the location." "Yes, do I need to bring anything?" "No need to bring anything we have plenty of food and drinks." "Your fine ass is enough!" "Great, were going to get dressed than pick up our two other friends LaToya and Tasha than head over." "Just give me an hour and I'll be there." "Cool, I'll see you soon, beautiful." Nia ends the call then contacts her other two friends to let them know the plans for tonight. Both ladies were happy and went to a party full of frat brothers. Everyone in the group of ladies was single, well kind of. Sarah situation was complicated if you asked her. If you asked me, she's single. "Put on Rihanna playlist while we get ready." "You know you have to do my make-up sis?" Said Sarah. "Yeah, I know." Nia was very talented and had numerous side hustles. She is a makeup artist for weddings and other celebrations. As well as a real estate agent, when she feels like it, mainly during the spring and fall when she's not too busy. "Open that bottle of pink Moscato and fill my glass up, I want to be nice by the time we get to the party." Said Nia. "What are you wearing tonight bitch?" asks Sarah. Nia replies, "I am wearing this tight black Gucci dress that hugs my curves with no panties and these 6-inch silver red bottoms." "Bitch! What are you wearing?" "Sarah jokingly says my birthday suit with this long brown trench coat." They both laughed. "I'm actually going to put on this Balenciaga shirt dress with these Balenciaga sneakers." "Just in case I need to run away from someone on the dance floor, who got stank breathe." "Giggles!" The two finish up getting ready, then head out the door to pick up their friends.

Upon on arriving at the event, Nia contacts Terrance. "Hey, me and my homegirls are here out in the parking lot ready to head to the door." "Great, I'm actually coming out to smoke I meet you at the door." "Okay." "He's coming out to meet us. Let me know what you all think of him." The ladies all proceed towards the entrance of the building. "There he goes ladies!" "What do you all think?" "That tall bald-headed man smoking?" Says LaToya. "Yes." "Well damn he fine as hell." Say LaToya and Tasha together. "Yes Ma'am, I hope his friends just as fine as he is!" Said Sarah. They all begin to laugh as they walk closer to the door. "Hey, is the party jumping?" Ask Nia. Tee replies, "You know it baby." "Hello, ladies how are you all doing tonight?" Collectively responds. Fine, thanks. "You got some single friends?" Ask Tasha. "Yeah, come on in let me introduce you all to a few of the fellas." Tee then puts his cigarette out and holds the door open for them. Once inside Tee waves his hand to his close fellow frat brothers who are his best friends. They then begin to move closer to Tee and the ladies. Fellas, I want you to meet some wonderful women I've recently met. "This here is Nia, she off limits, hopefully she'll let me take her out one day." Nia smiles. "These are her friends Sarah, Tasha and LaToya, you guys have fun Nia and I going to go catch up and get acquainted with one another. Ladies I hope you all enjoy and have a good time." Nia and Tee then walk away to grab something to drink and chat for a while. "So, tell me about yourself ma'am." Said Tee.

"Well, I come from a small family. I have an older sister and a little brother, I'm the middle child. Also known as the black sheep of the family. My parents raised my siblings and I to be very close knit, so we keep in touch with one another often. I don't have any kids; I am an auntie to two charming little boys and 1 beautiful little girl. I've been single for quite some time now, 4 years to be exact. By the way I think you may know me from the tv. I am news reporter for the local channel 3 news." "Oh, shit!" "Yes, you are on during the evening news, I watch you often beautiful." "Wow, you're a beautiful woman but much more attractive in person." says Tee, while licking his lips and undressing her with his big bug eyes. Nia then says, "enough about me handsome, tell me about you." "Well, I own and operate my own business. I'm a real estate broker, for the rich and wealthy. I mainly operate out of the Hampton Roads Virginia Beach area. I do have a child a daughter who is 5 from a previous marriage." "I've been married for 6 years divorce now for 7, been kind of a bachelor since then. I only had one relationship after my marriage, that lasted only a few months and I am looking for something serious." "I want to be off the market." They both laughed, chatted, and chuckled throughout the night. Nia was once again feeling very good and comfortable with this man. For her heart was broken twice in the past and she vowed not to date ever again. But somehow, she felt safe with this guy that she only knew for not even a whole day. Once again decided not to put a wall in between her and the new bae. When the party was over, they parted ways and vowed to keep in touch. Exchanged Instagram names, to make sure they will be in contact in some way. On the ride home Nia chatted all the way, telling the other ladies of the man she wanted to be with for sure. He was the perfect gentleman she had been praying and waiting for without a doubt. God has sent him her way.

The other ladies just listened as she talked away. For they were too drunk and sleepy to even reply. It was a good night for them all, the other ladies have men as well after all.

"Hawk"

Bold and fierce,

Brown feathers to the bone,

Yeah y'all, I got it all,

Doing what's right without breaking any laws.

Hunger creeps in, I must seek prey,

For the laws of nature,

I must obey.

So, I stay on path making sure not to stray,

Soon I'll strike gold and eat good one day!

Chapter 5: 2020

It's New Year's Day, January 1, 2020, Nia is a little hung over from the New Year's Eve party last night. Tee had proposed to her at the stroke of midnight, he's engaged to be married to a woman he thought he knew best. None the less, she gets out of bed to brush her teeth and wash her face. She smells breakfast being made; Tee is in the kitchen cooking fried potatoes, bacon, and eggs. Shortly after, she joins him in the kitchen, upon entering she yells "morning baby!" "Hey sweetheart, how are you this morning?" "I'm fine baby, just have a slight headache from drinking so much. I see you're doing well. Up making breakfast when you're normally still in bed." Said Nia, while smiling at her new fiancé. Tee leans in to give her a kiss while setting the table. He then replies, "Yes darling, I'm doing well and happy you want me to be your man." Tee then turns on r & b neo soul music by Maxwell and does a little dance, heads over to the stove and grabs the pot full of eggs. He put food on both plates and filled both their glasses with mimosa and they ate.

Later that evening the friend group met up with one another to have dinner at LaToya's & Steve's new home. By the way Steve is the guy LaToya met that night 3 years ago at the frat party, one of Tee's good friends. They got married in Vegas a year after they met. Tasha & Eric are together and share a lovely town home, they have been engaged for two years. Sarah got with Blake and left George all alone. Sarah & Blake are newlyweds, looking to buy their first new home together, plus they're expecting a baby girl very soon in 3 months. "What a wonderful home you have here!" Shouts Sarah, as LaToya shows them around. "Yes, it is! I'm going to need your brokers name and number; didn't you say she gotten you a great deal?" asked Tasha. "Yes, I will forward you her contact info, Mrs. Beverly know how to negotiate great deals." "3,000 square feet home for $350,000." Soon they joined the men in the dining room. The Carters had reserved a private chef for the night. For dinner, grilled blackened salmon, roasted red potatoes with garlic, fried seasoned asparagus with champaign and red wine to drink. "Umm, how delicious!" Says Blake as he tears into his salmon. "Yes, sir!" shouts Eric. "Compliments to the chef!" Yells Tasha. "I second that." Says Steve. "Have you all seen how the Coronavirus from China is now spreading all over into other countries?" Ask Nia. "Yes, I seen a few cases here in New York and California now." "Yells, out Blake." "This is serious I hope they contain it before it spreads more." "This is scary!" All agreed by nodding, as they continued to eat and chat the night away.

Three and a half months into the new year, the whole world comes to an abrupt stop. Stiffened by the Coronavirus or Covid19, major corporations, local businesses, restaurants, schools, and gyms were forced to shut down effectively immediately. The order called for all Americans to stay at home not to go out the house to any stores unless mandatory. Stay quarantined until further notice. If you do go out, make sure to wear a surgical or N95 mask with gloves. This displaced a lot of working-class Americans, plenty loss their jobs and where unable to pay mortgage, rent or any bills at all. The government knew too little about this virus and how it spreads from human to human. Nia contacts her parents because she wants to be close to them and make sure they stay safe. Her parents are much older now and she wants them to meet her new fiancé in person. "Hello Mom, how are you and dad?" "Hey sweetie we're doing just fine, here at the house unpacking groceries preparing for the lock down. How are you baby?" "I'm fine mom, thanks." "I want to come down spend some time with you both during the stay-at-home mandate." "Okay, sugar come on over." "I'm bringing Tee also; we have some news to share." "Great, your brother will be here as well with his family and so will your sister with hers." "Awesome so a family reunion!" Nia says giggling. "We'll be there later tonight, we're packing now." "Okay darling, see you soon. Bye" Nia gets off the phone with her mother and continued to pack while letting Tee know her siblings will be there with their extended families.

Nia contacts her friends to let them know about her plans and that Tee is coming along to meet the parents. Shortly after they packed the SUV and hit the road down south to Central Virginia. Along the way they stopped at Walmart to pick up so necessities as well as groceries, they didn't want to come empty handed. Soon they arrived at Nia's old childhood home, where she met her first lover and secretly conceived a child with. Unbeknown to her, Mateo was back home and planned to quarantine with his parents too, along with their unspoken of child. Nia and Mateo locked eyes for about five seconds upon Nia exiting the vehicle. "Hey Nia-Renee, it's been years since I've last seen you." She replies. "Yes, the summer before college, it has been about 28 years now." Mateo then ask, "are you here to stay with your parents during the lock down?" "I am, what about you?" "Yes, my little brother also, Javier." Javier is the child Nia and Mateo had conceived unknowingly to him. Nia didn't let him know she was pregnant; she was a scared 17-year-old girl at the time. She didn't want to jeopardize her future by becoming a mother even if she did make the choice to have sex. She did want to reap the consequences that came along. "Awe isn't that so wonderful of the two of you to take look after you parents." "Bella and Diageo should be coming as well." says Nia while quivering. "By the way this is my fiancé, Terrance." Terrance steps forward and say, "please to meet you man, you can call me Tee." "Cool, I'm Mateo or Mat." "I see you guys around soon; I need to get back in the house and clean out the basement." Terrance and Nia waves goodbye to Mateo and begin to unload the vehicle, soon knocking on her parents' door. Nia's father opens the door, overwhelmed with joy to see his baby girl. "Baby girl, look at you!" He hugs her tight and gives her a kiss on the cheek and invites them in. "Dad, mom this Terrance in the flesh." Her parents had only met him via the telephone.

"Hey Tee, how are you man?" Says Andre while shaking his hand and giving him a hug. "I'm well thank you sir." "Hey Mrs. East, how are you?" Tee leans over and hugs Mrs. East. "I'm doing wonderful, thank you." "Such a tall and handsome one you got here Nia." "You all make yourself comfortable and get settled in. I got some chili cooking in the crockpot and some cornbread in the oven." "The others should be here soon before dinner is ready." "Alright momma, we'll be back down shortly." Nia and Tee then take their belongings upstairs to Nia's old room. Got unpacked and came downstairs to join her parents.

The doorbell rings, it's Diageo with his wife Angela and 2 kids Junior and Angel. Nia yells, "I'll get it!" Nia opens the door, steps out, greets her little brother and family. "Hey little bro!" He isn't a little at all but a 6'3 man stronger than most. "Hey sis!" "Give me a hug!" They embrace one another, then hug the children and wife. "Come on in, Terrance, mom and dad are inside in the living kitchen preparing for dinner." "You guys, Diageo and family is here." They all come forward to greet them as well. Helped them down to the basement where they will be sleeping for their stay. Soon after the doorbell rang again. It was Bella-Rae, her husband and daughter, William, and Leah-Rae. Tee opens the door to meet Bella-Rae and her family for the very first time. "Hello, I'm Terrance, pleased to meet you, Bella, William and you must be Leah-Rae." "Hello!" They all greeted him back. Tee steps back and invites them in. Mom, Father, Nia, and Diageo step out of the kitchen runs to hug Bella. "It's about time you're here, shit I'm starving!" Says Diageo, jokingly while smiling. "You all will be staying upstairs in your old room and Leah will sleep in Diageo's old room." Said Mr. East. "Go ahead up and get settled in and come back down for dinner." Okay father we will be back down in five minutes. "Make it 2 minutes!" Shouts Diageo. "Oh, hush up boy, with your greedy self." "Take your time baby." "Diageo come on and set the table, Nia you go get the others and bring them to the table."

Bella, William, and Leah come down to dinner after unpacking. The entire family sits down for dinner. The adults at one table, the children at another. They laughed and exchanged stories about how life had been going for them all. Suddenly Nia bursts out and say, "I have an announcement to make you all." "Go ahead baby, what is it?" Said Mr. East. Nia holds up hands for everyone to see. Then, Terrance and Nia shouts, "we're getting married!" Everyone shouts with joy, "Congrats!" "Oh, baby I'm so happy for you!" "Thanks, Mama!" "I'm planning the wedding!" Shouts Mr. East jokingly. "Quiet, you can plan anything with me." Said Mrs. East while still smiling about the big news. "Well, we haven't set a date yet, we just got engaged on New Year's Eve." "Let me help plan it with you Nia? I want to pick the date, the colors, the venue, please, please, please." Ask Bella. "Sure sis." "Congratulation's man there's no returns, once you marry her, she's always yours now." Says Diageo to Tee. "Ha, ha, ha! That's fine, I have no plans on returning her. This time around will be forever, I will love her until death do us apart." "Aw!" They all said collectively, then raised their glasses and toasted. "You know I have a floral shop, so I am happy to do your bouquet and all other flower arrangements for your wedding." Says Angel. "Yes of course, plus I want that family discount." Says Nia, laughingly. "We got you sis." Replies Diageo. "Well, you all got plenty of time to sit and plan, it's no telling when this lock down mandate will be lifted." "However, when it does, I will be more than happy to marry you all as I am ordained as a minister as well." Says William. "Thank you all so much!" Says Nia, then she leans over and gives Tee a kiss on the lips. "Well, when the mandate is over, I think the date 2/22/22 would be perfect to commemorate you all special day. What do you guys think?" "Wow I like that, Bella!" Nia then turns to Tee and ask, "baby can we make that our day?" "I think it's enough time to iron out everything." "We have twenty-two and a half months until that day. We can do this, what do you think?" "Yes, perfect!"

"A Love Poem"

As the tides of the river

rise and fall,
I know you'll be here standing.
Six feet tall,
When the glacier on the mountains
begin to melt,
All the good, sweet loving
you give, I felt,
Like a Clydesdale in the wild
running wild and free,
Oh baby, baby, baby won't you come,
and be with me!

Chapter 6: Senior Year 1991

It was the last month of summer, just before my senior year of high school. I'd just turned 17 a month ago. It was hot a hell outside, 98 degrees to be exact, the fourth day this week to reach temperatures above 95. That didn't stop Sarah and I from going out to the public pool down at the recreational center. Over the years my body became shapelier and more voluptuous than ever. I was now shaped like a coke bottle, how Bella was in her high school days. I'd never dated because I was too afraid of what my papa would think. I wore a two-piece bathing suit to the pool which covered half of my ass, the center part. The other half was sticking out on the edges, showing some cheeks. My breast had grown to full D cup, but I had a small frame, waist was tiny with wide hips. On the way to the pool Sarah and I bumped into Mateo and his friends who were also headed the same way as us. Mateo had undergone puberty by now, he is 17 but looks like a grown man. Big muscle arms, nice chest, flat stomach lined with abs and a full mustache with beard. Mateo has finally caught Nia's eye and he knew she finally fancied him by the twinkle in her eyes. "Hey Nia!" "You young ladies heading to the pool?" "Yes." "Well so are we!" "May we all walk together?" "Sure Mateo!" Shouts Sarah. She had her eye on Mateo's best friend Jake and didn't want to miss the opportunity to mingle with him. "After the pool we're having a barbeque at my place. My parents are preparing for it now, by the time we get done swimming the food should be ready. You all are more than welcome to join us for some food and fun." Nia replies to Mateo. "Okay, I would love to stop by. Besides I love your mom's homemade guacamole, it's so tasty." "Well thanks! I'll be sure to let her know." They both smiled at one another as they all continued their walk to the pool. Once there, they all had a good time, jumping in and out of the water. Making cannon ball splashes, jumping off the diving board, playing Marco Polo and chicken fighting in the pool. That's when one person gets on the shoulder of another while in the pool, playing a fight with the other teamed up pair to knock the opponent off the shoulders of their teammate. Nia and Mateo were partners, Nia was on Mateo's shoulders, and they chicken fought their way to the top winning the game. Nia was so excited that she leaned over, while still on his shoulders and kisses Mateo on the lips. Mateo likes that of course. So, he moves Nia down off his shoulders and proceeded to kiss her more. "Uh oh, looks like these two have the hearts for one another!" Shouts out Timothy who is one of Mateo's friends. Timothy then horse play with Jake, imitating Nia and Mateo's make-out session. "Mateo what such beautiful eyes you have!" Said Timothy to Jake. Jake than says, "Nia what such gorgeous lips you have, I can kiss you all day!" The two then begin acting as if they are kissing and hugging. "Shut the hell up!" Says Mateo while laughing and splashing water on the two.

While walking home Nia and Mateo held hands and kissed along the way. "May I be your boyfriend, Nia?" "Yes, I would like that but only if you promise to stay a nice gentleman and walk me to and from class when school starts." "Of course, my love I will do anything for you beautiful!" They kissed again to seal the deal. "So, Sarah, are you seeing anyone?" asks Jake. "No, I've been single the whole summer since Adam pissed me off at the school carnival." "I would like to take you out sometimes, if that's ok with you." "I really enjoyed you today and would like to continue to have fun with you." "Yes, I would love that, Jake." She then pulls out a pen and writes her number on his muscle chest. "Cool!" Shouts Jake. They shortly arrived back at Mateo's parents' house and continued to horse play, dance, and eat the night away. Mateo and Nia enjoyed the last few weeks left in August, hanging out and being with one another every day. The two were inseparable, besides they lived directly across the street from one another, and their families were friends.

It's now September, school has been in session for one week now. Everyone at school and in the neighborhood where Nia & Mateo lived knew they were a couple. They were so affectionate with each other every time they got together to hang out. Holding hands, kissing, walking slowly through the hallways or on the block. One afternoon after school, the two were at Nia's house laying on the couch together watching midday tv. Mrs. East is at work at the hospital, Mr. East is upstairs sleeping, getting rest for his overnight shift later that night. Bella is away in college on campus at VSU, her parents' alma mater. Diageo is upstairs in his room doing his homework and watching cartoons. Mateo begins to kiss Nia and caresses her breast. The two make out on the couch touching and grabbing each other's genitals. "Damn you're hard! I never did this before Mat." "I know baby I want bad! I promise to go slow and be gentle." Says Mateo as he kisses her neck and puts his hands up her shirt and firmly cuffs her breasts. "Wait let's go downstairs in the basement." Whispers Nia. The two then head down to the basement. They go into the room further in the back locks the door, turn on the tv to BET because music videos were playing, and it would drown out the sound of their love making. Mateo slowly takes his shirt and pants off, leaving only his briefs on showing a huge bulge in the front. Nia takes a deep breath as he walks slowly towards her and begins to undress her. He lay her on the bed and began to kiss and caress her body. "Let me know if you want to stop and I will." "Okay, I will." Then Nia kisses Mateo and removes her bra and panties. They made gentle sweet love for about 10 minutes; it was over quick it was both their first time. This became their routine after school during the week. It was the only time they could sneak and be intimate.

The following month in October, Nia was surprised that her monthly cycle did not happen as usual. She thought to herself that her cycle must have changed. It's now November and still no menstrual cycle, plus she is moody, hormonal, and much hungrier than before. Still, she denied, overlooking what was happening to her body as her belly began to grow a little bit more. December came around and stomach grew even more, Mateo is starting to notice she is much thicker than before. "Baby, this holiday season got you eating a lot, but I like it you're much thicker and I love it, damn!" Shouts Mateo as he caresses her body and make love to her once more for the last time. Nia wants to end it, knowing she is pregnant but too afraid to share with anyone. The next day, however, she tells Sarah about her best friend. "Sarah, can you promise me to keep a secret?" "Sure, girl you know I want tell a soul if you don't want me too, what is it?" "I think I'm pregnant though I haven't been tested. I haven't had my cycle in 2 months now." "Let's go to the pharmacy to pick up an at home test. I took one last month myself. Thank you, God for it being negative!" Shouts Sarah while looking up at the sky and raising her hands giving the lord praise. She has been sexually active with Jake since meeting that hot summer day. "Okay but you go in and buy it, I'm too afraid." "No, problem babe I got you." They both get a ride to the pharmacy by Sarah older sister Asia, who is 23 years old and a college dropout who moved back home to work for her parents' business. The girls go to Sarah's home to take the test. 15 Minutes later a very light pink plus sign graced the front of the pregnancy test. "Oh shit!" Shouts out Nia. "Fuck, fuck, fuck!" Nia begins to cry. Sarah holds and consoles her reassuring her everything will be ok. "My sister can take you to have an abortion if you would like. All you need is $300, and it will go away, and no one would know, that procedure is confidential." "I don't know, I'm too scared." Says Nia while sobbing on the bathroom floor.

New Year's come its now 1992, halfway through January and 4 months pregnant; Nia hides her stomach wearing big clothes. Plus, she works out and eats much healthier, trying not to get too big for anyone to notice. She Attends all the school senior events, commencement, senior skip day, annual school cookout. She continued writing for the school newspaper and earned a scholarship to cover all four years at Howard

University. She went on to graduate top of her class but didn't go to the beach the night of graduation with her friends. She wouldn't enjoy herself that much, plus her ex-boyfriend Mateo was still around a part of her graduating class. Instead, she stayed home eating and celebrating with her family, Bella was back in town after completing her sophomore year at college. "Nia, you are getting big girl, I thought mama was joking but she wasn't playing around." Says Bella. "I know this holiday weight I can't seem to shake, but this summer before I start college, I'll be thin like the summer before." "I can work you out if you want me to. My friends and I normally would work out every day on campus but since I'm here you'll be my workout buddy for the summer." "Yes, that would be great I would love that, it will keep me motivated to have a partner." "Alright now, I get up a 6am to start my morning and I'm working out by 7am." "Say less, I get up every morning by 6 anyway. I'm used to getting up and ready for school, plus making sure Diageo is up eating before I leave." The next day the two sister's workout with one another, for about a week straight. Bella's college boyfriend wants to take her to Michigan to meet his parents, so she leaves with him to stay for a month. That evening Nia goes over to Sarah's house, while laying on Sarah's bed chatting and eating popcorn making future. Suddenly Nia's water breaks. Nia begins to feel pain all over her body, mostly in her stomach. The two girls look at one another and simultaneously say, "oh shit! It's time!

"Dream"

To have a dream

To enjoy the cream

I wonder what just may come of me?

Could I conquer the bee?

Would I just travel the seven seas?

Should I hope and lather my brain with pain?

Or stand proud and speak my name just in vain?

You see, to have a dream and not succeed,

One could only imagine what life would be!

Chapter 7: Sarah

Sarah Menahem is Nia's best friend, who happens to be white. Her family welcomed the Easts' when they first moved to the neighborhood. Her father, Adam, 40, has been the sheriff for the county for the last 5 years. Prior to being elected as the county's sheriff, he was a police officer for the city of Richmond for 19 years. Lucy, her mother who is also 40, worked at the county town hall as a tax collector upon finishing high school. They also have their own business, a small floral shop and four beautiful children. Two girls and a set of twin boys to be exact. Asia, 20, wanted freedom from her parents is far away at college at the university of Iowa. Sarah is 14, the middle child amongst her siblings. The boys are 7 and very active, full of energy and attend school with Diageo. Her family is very religious, they are catholic, and her parents make sure every day to bestow the teachings that come along with the religion onto the kids. Sarah is a little reluctant to follow the catholic rules but play the part when in front of her family. She is boy crazy and very popular with the guys; she has been performing fellatio on the boys in her class since the 8th grade. Now a freshman in high school, she carried her salacious acts into her high school years. Once before after football and cheerleading practice, she performed her act on a few of the guys underneath the bleachers. You should've seen them lined up waiting on their turn to see if the rumors they've heard about her in the locker room were true. Well, it was true, and she didn't care what others thought of her. Most guys liked her and that's all that mattered now.

After that eventful day, Sarah told Nia all about her experience behind the bleachers. "You wouldn't believe what happened today after practice." "What happened?" "Let's just say that I did what I do best when I'm in the mood for a little fun." "Which is?" "Well, some of the guys now call me the fellatio queen." She says very proudly, and both burst out into laughter. "No, seriously?" "But who did you do it with?" "Tom, Steve, Josh, Dejuan, and Derrick. They said they wanted to see if I could live up to my reputation, plus I wanted too." "I enjoyed every minute of it." The girls burst out laughing again. "What a slut!" "Thank you, bitch!" They laughed again. Sarah is standing in the mirror in Nia's room fixing her hair. "You know Josh wants me to come over tonight when his parents go out tonight. He must babysit his little brother for a few hours and wants me to keep him companied." "Are you going to go over?" "Hell yeah!" "Josh is hot, and I think he wants to go all the way." "Are you afraid to do that?" "No, you have to lose it at some point." "I'm ready to step up to the big league and play with the big boys." "Besides, I've been sucking since middle school, I want to try something new and exciting." "Any way when you are going to find someone and become a young woman?" "I don't know?" "I'm too afraid." "Such a chicken, you know you can't let fear control your life, that's not living." "I know." Nia sighs.

Later that night Sarah goes over to Josh's house after his parents head out for the night. "Hey, come on in." "My parents just left; they will be gone for a few hours." "Cool!" "I made us some popcorn for us to watch a movie tonight on the couch." "My little brother is actually at Steve's house, playing with his little brother for a while." "So, were here alone?" "Yeah, baby." Sarah smiles then proceeds to kiss Josh on the lips, tonging him down in a rage of passion. They head to the couch in the living room and get right to it. They both enjoyed it so much they did it twice that night. They never watched that movie or eat ate the popcorn. After going at it like two teens who never did it before; Josh bursts out and say, "I want you to be my girlfriend." Sarah replies in a happy but victorious way, "Okay!" Sarah didn't want to really be with Josh but just wanted to have him under her spell so she could manipulate him sometimes. She liked doing that with all the guys she ever dated, she had a control issue since she couldn't be herself out loud in the present of her family.

Once Sarah got home, showered, and settled in, she contacted Nia via the telephone to tell her all about her night with Josh. "So, how was it? Was it good? Was it everything you expected? Would you go over again?" Sarah laughs and says, "come down now little one." "Yes, it was great, I really enjoyed it. I enjoyed it so much we did it twice." "Really?" "Yeah, he asked me to be his girlfriend and I said yes. But if he buys me lunch at school." "Wow!" Nia was very surprised at how Sarah can control the mind of a 15-year-old boy." "I think I'm going to date him for a few months until I get tired of him and then move on to the next." "I don't want to be with him forever, just for now." "You know guys this age only thinks about one thing, so it's very easy to manipulate them, if you know what you are doing." The girls continued the conversation throughout the night. Sarah dated Josh for four months and then started dating Tom soon after. Sarah was never single and if she was it wasn't for long. A guy was always around lurking or trying to get with her even if she had a boyfriend. She was the talk of the locker room, and all the boys wanted a turn with her.

In the spring of 1989 while finishing up her freshman year in high school, Sarah becomes pregnant. She didn't panic because she knew she could count on her older sister Asia who has completed her junior year at college and is back at home for the summer. "Asia, I have to tell you something, but you have to promise not to tell mom and dad." "Let me guess, you're pregnant, aren't you?" says Asia with a little smirk on her face. "Yes, but please don't say anything, I want you to help me get an abortion." "I have the money for the procedure, I got it from Tom. It's his baby but neither one of us want to keep it." "Okay, I want say anything, I'll make the appointment and we can go together." "By the way, you're not talking about Thomas Smith. Gregory younger brother?" "Yes, I actually am." "Oh shit, talk about déjà vu." A few years back Asia and Gregory were in the same predicament and chose to abort their baby also. "After the procedure you will be a little tired so you'll have to rest, I'll take off of work so I can help you throughout the day." "Thank you so much Asia, I really appreciate this." "No, problem just don't make the same mistake twice." "I promise, I won't!" Sarah decided not to tell Nia about her mishap, of how she wasn't being safe and making sure not to get pregnant. She hardly used protection, especially if it was someone she really liked.

That following weekend the two sisters went to the abortion clinic to have the deed done. They never told anyone. However, that summer right after her 15th birthday, Sarah found herself in the same predicament as before but this time it's Dejuan's baby. Sarah again sought out her sister for help. "Asia, please don't judge me but I need your help again." "Goddamn it, girl!" "I told you to be careful!" "Don't you kids know what a condom is?" "Yes, but I really don't like the feeling with one. Plus, he normally would pull out in time." "Please, don't judge me right now. Just help!" "Okay, but this is it. I can't keep helping you out if you're going to keep getting pregnant. Next time use a condom!" "Do you have the money so I can schedule the appointment?" "Yes, and I promise this is the last time." Asia makes the appointment for that upcoming weekend. Sarah is supposed to go with Nia to swimming lessons at the YMCA, but she'll have to sit this one out.

The next day Nia contacts Sarah to make sure they are still on for the weekend. "Sarah don't forget we have swimming lessons on Saturday at the YMCA and Mateo will join us as well." "Uh, I actually wouldn't be able to make it this Saturday Nia." "Why not? Is everything okay?" "Yeah, well, not quite but it will be after this weekend." "What's wrong? You know I'm your girl, you can tell me anything I promise not to say a word." "I'm pregnant and Asia is taking me to the clinic to have an abortion." "Say, what? Shut your mouth, you're kidding with me, right?" "No, I wish I was, but this isn't the first time either. A few months back I was pregnant with Tom's baby and now Dejuan's." "Damn! See that right there is why I'm so scared." "I can understand that, but when you do cross that line just make sure to use a condom." The girls laughed and continued to chat as Sarah told Nia about the clinic and the whole procedure to abort the embryo.

Saturday arrived Sarah went on to correct her mistake for the second time. Nia and goes over to Mateo house to make sure he is up and ready to head out. "Mateo are you ready for the day?" "Do you even know how to doggy paddle?" "No, but I'll learn. I'm sure it can't be that hard." Mateo is secretly in love with Nia but a little shy to say so. "It's very to learn, you'll be ok, hopefully." "What do you think about the new Terminator movie?" Asks Nia. "It was awesome, filled with action. The Terminator kicked some ass!" Says Mateo while laughing. "You should go with me to the movies next weekend to see Back to the Future the sequel." "Sure, if I can bring Sarah along, I don't want you thinking this is a date." Says Nia while laughing at Mateo because of course he wanted a date with Nia, and she knew it. However, she wasn't ready to date and was still kind of shy. The next weekend the three of them went to the movies and had fun. They became the three amigos that day and throughout their high school days.

"I.Q."
Don't you ever forget,
Failure builds character.
It is a learning process,
Never give up,
Not even on your worst day!
You must push through,
Make adjustments, if it doesn't serve you!

Chapter 8: Javier Rodriguez

On the night of June 27, 1992, the doorbell rang. Mr. Rodriguez jumps up to rush to the door. The family had just finished eating dinner and were in the living room discussing Mateo plans to head off to NYU for the upcoming fall. "Who is it?" Asks Mr. Rodriguez, but no response. He then opens the door and looks down to see a baby sitting in a basket, wrapped in a hand towel. "My God, someone has left a baby at the door!" "What?" Shouts the whole family. Mr. Rodriguez picks up the basket with the baby in it and brings it inside. Quick contact the police, we must make them aware of what has happened. Mrs. Rodriguez called out to the authority. Upon arrival they take the baby to the hospital to be checked out. Mr. and Mrs. Rodriguez decide to hop in their car and follow the police to the hospital. While on their way they say a prayer and begin to discuss the future of this new life that was left upon their doorstep. Vowing to adopt the child and raise it as their own and they did just that.

While Mateo went off to college his old room became Javier's. When Nia went away for college she stayed away. Never really came back home the only time she visited was for Christmas and only stayed for 3 days at the most. She didn't want to run it to her own child that lived directly across the street from her parents. Nonetheless, Javier was unaware that he was adopted, he looked just like the family and fitted right in. The Rodriguez gave him a wonderful life and put him through college like they did for the other biological children.

On the morning of April 1, 2020, Javier got up early around 6am to make his family breakfast. He will soon be 30 in just a couple of months. While preparing such a huge breakfast he realized he ran out of butter and decided to knock on the East's door to see if they had any to spare. "Ding Dong." "Senior, senorita East, it's Javier from across the street. "Ding Dong." "I'm coming!" Shouts Nia, as her whole family sleeps. Nia jumps out of bed, throws on her robe, and heads downstairs to the front door. She opens the door and stands there in shock looking into Javier's big brown eyes like his father and beautiful smile like his mother. "Hello, I'm Javier Mr. & Mrs. Rodriguez's youngest son. I don't think we formally met. You're Nia, correct?" Nia stands there for a few seconds and then responds. "Yea, yes, I'm Nia." "Pleasure to meet you, I only heard a few stories about you from your parents and Mateo." Nia smiles. "Well, I hope they were all good things." "Yes, senorita, nothing but wonderful things." "I'm making breakfast for my family and ran out of butter." "I was wondering if you're parents had any to spare?" "Yes, just give me a moment Javier, let me grab that for you." Javier nods. Nia runs off into the kitchen to grab the butter but then starts to cry for a second. She wipes her face and returns to the door with two sticks of butter. "Here you are, this should hold you until you all go out to the market." "Thank you so much senorita, I'll see you around." "You're welcome, bye!" Nia shuts the door and Javier heads back home to finish cooking.

Later that day Javier checks his email and sees that his results are in from his Christmas present Lucia has got him. It was a DNA kit from Ancestry, and he finally decided to use it about 8 weeks ago. Lucia was aware that Javier wasn't her biological brother and thought that everyone should know where they came from. Lucia never informed the rest of the family of her decision to purchase the gift, she kept it a secret and told Javier to do so as well. Upon reading his results, which was very shocking to his surprise. For his paternal lineage, it showed that Lucia may be his sister and parents as grandparents. On the maternal side it showed Bella-Rae and Diageo as aunt and uncle. Javier was stunned, puzzled at the results. "This can't be right!" He grabs his sister Lucia, and they go off into his room and shut the door. "Look at these results this can't be right, right?" Lucia analyzes the results. She was just as puzzled as Javier. Not because he wasn't her brother as she already knew that, but because they do share some of the same blood. "Wait a minute, let me grab Mateo." Lucia runs off and comes back with Mateo. "Look at this Mateo." "What is this?" "It's DNA results on Ancestry." "It shows Javier is related to us biologically." "Well, I am right?" "I'm you all youngest brother?" Mateo and Lucia look at one another than sigh. Lucia then says, "I'll explain it to him, I am the one who opened pandora's box." Lucia then explains to Javier how he came to them. Upon explaining Lucia is hit with an epiphany. She turns to Mateo and asks, "have you and the Nia been sexually intimate with one another as teenagers?" "Yes." "At any point did she become pregnant?" "No, she never said anything and if she would've been she would have said something." "I'm going to have you take a test also, I'll pay for it." "Okay." Lucia proceeds to order the test online. "We must keep this amongst ourselves until we figure out the rest. "Okay, sure." says Mateo and Javier.

The next week the package arrived for Mateo to spit into a tube and mail it back. He did exactly just that, immediately. It's now the first week of June and the results are in. Mateo quickly grabs Lucia and Javier. They all went down to the basement to the room where Mateo had been sleeping for the last two months. "My results are back; I'm logging in so we can all see together. After analyzing the results, the three couldn't believe what they were seeing. It showed Mateo has Javier's father and someone linked to the East's bloodline as the mother. Nia-Renee hasn't taken an Ancestry DNA kit, only her other two siblings have. "Oh my god!" Shouts Mateo while shaking his head. "We must inform mom and dad." Shouts Lucia. "So, you're my father and not my brother?" asks Javier, with a concerning disbelief on his face. "I may be, I do apologize I had no idea." "Let's head back upstairs and inform the rest of the family." Says Lucia. They all head back up and Lucia calls out to her parents. "Mami, pappi come quick, we have somethings to discuss." As their parents enter the living room, there mother ask, "what is it my dear?"

"Yeah, why are you yelling sweetheart?" "Come take a sit I have a few things I want to explain to the both of you." "I purchased Javier a DNA kit for Christmas, because I wanted him to know where he came from." "You did what?" "Who do you think you are to make such a big decision for this family?" "I am your father and the patriarch of the family. Which means I make the decisions on what is best for us all, if I am well and breathing. Do you understand me?" "Yes, father but this is important. I believe if you want to know where you are headed in life, you must know where you come from." "Dios mio! Estos ninos me van an enviar a una tumba temprana!" Says Mr. Rodriguez, while shaking his head and putting his hand over his forehead. Lucia begins to explain the results and informs them that Javier is related to them through Mateo. "He's not your son but grandson. Nia-Renee maybe his mother but we will need to test her to be certain." "I can't believe all of this, but it makes since why every interaction with her she stares at me quietly, as if she is analyzing me. Mateo stands up and shouts, "I will bring this to her attention, I will have the conversation with her immediately!" Mrs. Rodriguez chimes in. "Not today, we will wait until tomorrow. Today has brought enough surprises." "Yes, Mami." The family then embraces Javier and assures him nothing will change. "You are one of us, always has been, always will be my love." says Mrs. Rodriguez.

It's now three months into the pandemic, most items such as toilet paper, disinfection wipes and numerous other food items are missing from store shelves. Americans are buying up just about everything while on lockdown. Many factories and production companies have slowed or halted its production. It's Javier's 30th birthday, which he must celebrate amongst his family in their home. The family decided to have a barbeque in the backyard and celebrate with the little items they were able to get from the store. Javier isn't his normal jolly self because the idea of his biological mother living directly across the street haunted him. He begins to ask himself some questions to try to understand why one would do what Nia has done. He can't come to a concrete answer which reinforces the unsettling feeling in his body. "I want to go over and knock on the door and demand answers!" "No, Javier baby." "I know this has got to be so challenging for you but also it must be challenging for her also." says Mrs. Rodriguez. "I will contact Mrs. East tomorrow to see if we all can sit down outside." "We'll have a panic while socially distancing ourselves and discuss the issue at hand." Javier begins to cry. "No, baby don't cry, it's going to be just fine." "Yes, I know Mami. I'm just emotional right now. Even though you all are my family, just not in the order which I grew up believing." "Mateo, I don't know if I can call you dad, it feels weird." "It all feels weird to me too. I can't believe she would do such a thing. I just don't know what to think of her now, I don't view her the same anymore." Mateo then breaks down and cries. Mr. Rodriguez stands up and say, "we are a strong family here, this will not break us but make us even stronger!" He then walks over to his mother Maria and grabs her hand. "My father, may he rest in peace Luis Rodriguez are one of the toughest men I've ever known. He has taught me plenty of lessons. One of them is to not shy away from fear but to walk through it to get to the other side." "We will get through this together as a family, because together as a unit we are hermetic, we will persevere."

"CONFUSION"

Confusion invades my mind and body,
Taking over like a disease.
One that I can't seem to freeze.
As I lay on the bed,
Trying to find what's next ahead.
I'm in it for the long haul,
Even though I keep seeming to fall.
I will never give up!

No, not at all!

Chapter 9: Pain!

Nia is on the floor crying, screaming, she's in labor and frightened, she doesn't know what to do. Sarah is panicking, pacing back and forth. "Asia will be here soon; she'll be able to help us. She was studying to be a nurse; she can deliver the baby." "Ouch, ouch!" Nia begins to take deep breaths in between the contraction pains hoping that will help alleviate it. Asia arrives and walks through the front door and hears Nia screaming. She runs upstairs unaware of what is going on. She calls out to Sarah. "Sarah? What's going on in there?" Asia opens the door to see Nia on the floor with no pants or undergarment on. "Asia she's in labor ready to give birth! Please help!" "Oh shit!" "Okay, okay, just breathe very slowly and calmly I don't want you to panic, it's going to be alright." "Sarah, go downstairs put a pot of water on the stove to boil. Grab the biggest pot you can; on your way back up grabs some towels and some rags." "Okay!" Sarah runs down and does exactly what Asia say. "Just breathe, count to three and take deep breaths." Nia does just that and screams whenever she feels the baby sliding down through her uterus. "Oh my god you're stating to crown the baby is coming!" "Sarah!" "Come quickly, bring the rags and towels." Sarah soon enters and places the towels next to Asia. "Just go grab the water even if it's not boiling yet, I'm sure it's hot." "Also, bring up a bowl, fill it with cold water." "I want you to hold her hand and to keep her cool by putting a rag in the cold water and placing it on her forehead." "Do you understand?" "Yes." "Good." "Listen to me Nia I'm going to count to ten and you push every time on ten." "Yes, I will!" Asia counts out loud to ten, Nia pushes once at ten. They repeat the process five times, and on the last push the baby head is fully visible, and Sarah tells Nia to push again, and she pulls the baby out. Sarah clears the baby's airway with her fingers and the baby begins to cry out.

"Great job Nia, it's a boy!" Sarah follows the lessons and teachings she received while in college. She cleans the baby boy up and wraps him in a towel and hands him to Nia. Nia is so confused and very emotional at this point because she doesn't know what to do. She knows that she can't keep the baby because her dream of going to college will be just that, a dream. She begins to cry out as she looks at her baby boy. "What's wrong?" asks Sarah. "Well, she I can't keep him. My parents did not know I was pregnant, nor did Mateo." "So, what are you going to do?" "Do you want to drop him off at the fire station?" "No, I don't want to leave him with strangers." "I'm thinking of leaving him with his father's family." "The Rodriguez family, I think will raise him like their own." "They are good loving people." "Okay Mateo does know, right?" "Yes, I'm just going to leave him at the door, ring the bell runoff, hide and watch them take him in." Nia burst out crying again, not really wanting to do that but she feels as if it is the right thing to do in her situation. All three girls cleaned up the mess and did exactly what Nia plan. Afterwards, they made an agreement to keep what happened tonight a secret amongst them, never to speak of it again.

The next morning, Mrs. Rodriguez visits Mrs. East and tells her all about last night on how a baby was left at their doorstep. Mrs. Rodriguez calls it a miracle a blessing that God has chosen her to be this baby's mother. "You say what?" "Someone left a baby at your doorstep last night?" "Oh, sweet Jesus!" "I wonder why they chosen your door." "How is the baby?" "He is fine very healthy. My husband and I are going to adopt him and name him Javier." "Oh, bless your heart what a sweet thing to do!" Mrs. East leans in and hugs Mrs. Rodriguez. "If you all need anything please don't hesitate to ask." "Andre and I will be of any assistance; your family has been wonderful and kind to us." "Thank you so much Cynthia!" "Of course, it's the least we can do." Mrs. East walks

Mrs. Rodriguez to the front door. "You all should come over and see the baby later today before your husband heads to work." "Yes, we will stop by, and I will bake a strawberry cake to celebrate the new addition to your family." "Okay, great! See you later" "Bye!" Mrs. East shuts the door and calls out to her family. "Honey!" "Nia, Diageo!" "Come downstairs quick I have some news to share. They all come into the living room and grab seats. "What is it baby?" Asks Andre. "Mrs. Rodriguez just left and informed me of some surprising news." "Someone has left at baby at her doorstep last night, a newborn to be exact." "Oh no!" Shouts out Mr. East while placing his hand over his mouth. "What are they going to do?" "Well, they took the baby to the hospital to get checked out and he is healthy." "She said her family will keep the baby and adopt him." "I told her we will be over later today see the new addition bestowed upon them." "Okay, great, did they need anything?" "She didn't say, but I did let her know we will be more than happy to help, if so." "Alright honey." Mr. East walks over and kisses his wife. "I'm going to start preparing this cake I promised to bring when we stop by." "Nia, baby is everything ok?" Nia is sitting in shock with a blank stare on her face. Feeling very scared trying to stay calm. "Yes, everything is fine." "I just was thinking how someone can just leave their baby at a random person's door." "I don't know, but we are not the family that judges others." "I can only imagine how scared the parents must be or what they might have gone through to do such a bizarre thing." "Mrs. Rodriguez looks at it as a miracle and blessing." "How wonderful of her they are such good people." says Andre while walking out of the living room and back upstairs. The rest of the family exit the living room as well and go on with their day.

Around five in the evening the East family all head over to the Rodriguez's to celebrate baby Javier. Mr. East knocks on the door. "Knock, knock, knock." Mr. Rodriguez opens the door. "Hola!" "Hey man, we came over to see the baby." "Your lovely wife stopped over earlier and invited us over." "My wife baked you all a strawberry cake." Mrs. East hands Mr. Rodriguez the cake. "Thank you so much Mrs. East!"

"You all come on in and have a seat." "I'll grab my family." Mr. Rodriguez places the cake in the kitchen and calls out to his family. They all come into the living room, grab a seat as Mrs. Rodriguez then enters with the baby. "Oh my!" "What a beautiful baby!" "I wonder why someone would do this." Says Mrs. East. "I don't know but he's ours now and we're going to love him like our own." says Mrs. Rodriguez as she kisses the baby on the forehead. "What are you all going to name him?" Asks Nia. "Javier Emanual Rodriguez!" shouts Mr. Rodriguez. "What a great name champ!" shouts Mr. East. They all take turns holding the baby and admiring him except for Nia. She doesn't want to get too close or too attached. Afterall she is holding a secret that she must keep from seeing the light of day. They then ate Mrs. East's strawberry cake and drank Mrs. Rodriguez homemade lemonade.

The next day, Nia invites Mateo over to chat with him and see how he feels about his new little brother. "How do you feel about your new little brother?" "I think it's cool, another sibling to teach how to play sports." "Plus, I'm painting my room and making it his since I'm heading to college in the fall." "That's nice of you!" "You always been a nice positive guy." "That's what made me fall for you." "Are you falling now?" The two burst out laughing. "No, big head." "I don't want to date anymore; I just want to go away to college and explore." "Besides, we're going to different schools, and I know they're going to be plenty of beautiful ladies at Florida A&M University." "Yeah, you right." There are its one of the reasons why I'm choosing to attend to be honest." The two laughed again. "You see, you guys always worried about woman." "What are you going to major in?" "I don't know I think I want to become a football coach." "What are you going to major in at Howard?" "I'm thinking Journalism or Mass communications." "I'm not sure, hopefully I will figure it out after a semester or two." "Whatever I chose, it has to be centered on me writing or creating something." "Are you going to keep in touch while away?" Asks Mateo. "Maybe, I don't want to be too distracted and flunk out." "But I will visit home for the Christmas holiday only." "Damn girl, it sounds like you're trying to run away." Nia laughs. "I am." "From what?" "This country lifestyle." "I want to be back in the city and amongst socialites." "I want to have a career where I can call the shots and interview people while at lunch or out at a major event." "Sounds like you want to be a reporter." "Probably, who knows what life have in store for any of us." "True, let's make a promise to visit each other at least once while away at school." "I'll come to D.C. to see you and you will come to Florida, when you can." "Okay, that sounds like a good plan." "That may be my first spring break destination since you're near the beach with clear blue water." "Sweet!" "Pinky promise?" "Yes, pinky promise." The two then lock pinkies, vowing not to break their promises. Mateo stretched and yarns. "I'm starving!" "My mom is making meatloaf with gravy, mashed potatoes, corn on the cob and fresh collard greens if you want to stay for dinner." Says Nia. "Hell yeah!" "I love your moms' cooking." "Okay, I'll let her know you will be staying." This was the last time the two sat and had a conversation as friends for the summer. The two were heading off to college in a month. They both chose to work the remaining days of summer to save and have money while away from home. Nia never went back over to the home of the Rodriguez family to visit baby Javier. If she wanted to move forward with the decision she had made and not feel guilty, she had to stay far away. So, she thought. She didn't know that this was only suppressing the issue and not actually a solution. Just a temporary band aid.

"You must!"

You must achieve your goals,

You must find the roads,

That will guide your soul,

To a world filled with Diamonds and gold.

To get here you must transpire,

So, get inspired, by the words,

Get empowered by the words,

So, you can fly high, above the birds,
Even though it feels as if life is on hold,
Because you never ever been told,
Your black is beautiful, brilliant, and bold.
Well, I'm here to let you know,
You're Amazing, dazzling, talented,
So, let it glow!

Chapter 10: The Meeting

On the morning of June 28, 2022, Mrs. Rodriguez gets up at 7am and prepares breakfast for her family like any other day. She has a large family, so she prepares a large meal and squeezes oranges for her homemade orange juice. She didn't have to yell out to her family to come down to eat. They can smell the aroma of freshly made pancakes, bacon, corn beef hash, fried potatoes, eggs, and mama's blueberry biscuits in the air. One by one they all came and entered the kitchen, grabbed a seat as Mrs. Rodriguez set the food upon the table. Mrs. Rodriguez sat at one end of the table as Mr. Rodriguez sat at the other end and said grace before chowing down. No one said a word during breakfast, only ate. Everyone was nervous as today was the day of reviling the truth. After eating, Mrs. Rodriguez phones Mrs. East. "Hello Cynthia, its Marisol, how are you this morning my love?" "I'm wonderful, thanks for asking. How are you today?" "Not so good, my family and I have come to a shocking revelation." "Are we able to set up a meeting some time today, to discuss some important information with your family?" "Yes, sure!" "May I know what it may entail?" "Well, it's pertaining to Javier." "I would like to wait until everyone is together to go over any details?" "Please keep calm and gather your family but don't let them know anything." "Okay, well how does noon sounds?" "That's perfect I will see you then, goodbye for now." "Alright, see you later."

At 11am Marisol is preparing lunch for the family. She normally doesn't do this; she would only prepare breakfast and dinner for the family. However, because of the looming thoughts that something may go wrong at the meeting, she wants her family to be comfortable and at ease. It's very odd and unusual that something so heinous occurs in their neighborhood or family. Mrs. Rodriguez wants to properly prepare her family for the day and start off by feeding them. While eating the cold cut sandwiches and chips Marisol provided, she begins the conversation with her family about how the day would proceed. "I have contacted Mrs. East to let her know we all would be stopping by to talk at noon." "I have informed her that it is important, and her family will need to be present as well." "I did not discuss any details on what we would be discussing." "She agreed so, I will need for you all to be polite and open minded as we navigate through this uncomfortable conversation today." "Yes ma'am," replies the whole family. "Your father and I will lead the conversation first." "If at anytime either one of you would like to say something or ask a question, do not hesitate but please do not speak over anyone." "That can make the situation hostile, we are not looking to hurt or shame anyone but to gain an understanding." "Javier, do you have any questions?" "No, I just want to the bottom of it." "I understand and we will." "Mateo, is there anything you would like to say?" "Yeah, can we pray before heading over I have this crazy feeling in my stomach." "Sure, of course baby," replies Marisol. The family finishes their lunch and says a prayer to help guide them through such a difficult but much needed conversation with the East's.

Over at the East's home, Mrs. East calls her family to the living room. "I've received a disturbing phone call today from Mrs. Rodriguez and she wants to stop by with her family to discuss a few things." "What exactly she wants to discuss, I have no idea, but she said it is imperative." Nia begins to fill a little sick to her stomach, not knowing what the Rodriguez's want and not wanting to see Javier, her little secret. "What time will they be coming over?" Nia asks. "We agreed upon twelve noon." Mrs. East looks down at her watch on her wrist. "So, in five minutes to be exact." Nia stomach begins to tighten, she jumps up to run out to the bathroom. "Excuse me for a moment." In the bathroom Nia looks at herself and begins to cry and talk to herself. "Okay, you can do this Nia." "You can get through this today, just like you have before." "You are strong, brave and intelligent." "You got this!" Nia splashes water on her face and wipes it dry with a hand towel before rejoining her family in the living room. Upon entering the living area and grabbing the seat next to her fiancé, the doorbell rang. "Ah, they are here!" "Honey, can you grab the door?" Mrs. East asked Mr. East. "Sure baby!" Andre gets up and opens the door. "Hello, my dear neighbor." "How are you all today?" "We've seen better days but we're thriving," says Mr. Rodriguez. "How are you and your family?" "We are doing just fine." "Come on in, my family is in the living room." "We've been expecting you all." The Rodriguez's steps inside, heads to the living room and greets the East's. Andre shuts the door behind the last member to enter the home. "May I get you all anything to drink?" Asks Mr. East. "No, we're fine, thank you," replies Mr. Rodriguez. "So, what's going on?" "How can my family and I assist today?" Mr. Rodriguez begins to explain. "We are not here to start any trouble; we are just here to gain some clarity." "My family and I have gained knowledge of Javier's original family." Nia sighs. "Okay, great!" "Have you all met them yet or informed?" Says Mr. East. "That's why we are here." Nia begins to break down crying, sobbing on the floor. "Baby, what's wrong?" Ask Mrs. East as she bends down and lifts Nia up. Nia then sobs in her mother's arms with her face lying on her mother's chest. "I know this may be challenging for you Nia," says Mrs. Rodriguez. "However, its only fair that we inform you all of the knowledge that we possess." "What are you say?" Shouts Bella. Lucia begins to explain all about the DNA testing kit they've taken for Ancestry. Bella and Diageo are familiar with the testing kit because they have taken one as well. "The results concluded that Javier is actually related to us." "He is my nephew and Mateo's son." "The results also showed that you and Diageo are his aunt and uncle." The whole East family stops in and looks at one another in disbelief. "How can that be?" Shouts Diageo. "Are you saying Nia is his mother?" Nia begins to sob louder. Javier then begins to break down. Mrs. Rodriguez grabs Javier and consoles him. "Wait a minute, so are you telling me he is Nia's son?" Asks Mr. East. "Yes, sir," replies Mateo. "Nia and I as you all know dated while in high school, but I did not know that she was pregnant." "Nia, baby is this true?" Mrs. East's asks her daughter. "Yes, mama, I'm sorry!" Says Nia while still crying. "It's okay baby, but tell us when you had the baby and how you were able to hide this from us?" Nia wipes her face and begins to explain to everyone in the room. She informed them that she took a pregnancy test back in the beginning of her last year in high school and broke up with Mateo not informing him of the positive results. She explained that her best friend Sarah was always aware and helped her keep the secret. "Sarah and Asia were with me the night of June 27, when I gave birth to him and helped me deliver." "The three of us then cleaned him up, wrapped him in a towel and placed him on the doorsteps of the Rodriguez's home that night." "I was so afraid; I did not know what to do!" "I thought you and papa would disown me or kick me out of the house." "I did not want to throw away my dreams of going to college and becoming a journalist." "Instead, I got rid of the baby in the safest way to my knowledge at the time." "Oh, sweetie your mother and I would've never done such a thing." "You are our child." "I have failed you, if you believed we would do that." Mr. East turns to the Rodriguez family and say, "I do apologize, I am actually speechless." "Javier, this means I am your grandfather, and I will embrace you as my grandson." "If you would allow me to enter your life." Javier responds, "yes sir." Nia wipes her face and walks closer to Javier and Mateo. "I am so sorry to the both of you." "I was just a confused seventeen-year- old girl, I thought I was making the right decision." Mateo begins to cry and said, "I do forgive you." "I just wish you would've told me something, so we could've worked through it together." "I would've stepped up and been the man my father has raised me to be today." "I do thank you for leaving him at my doorstep, because I was still able to be a part of his life." Javier starts to cry again, becoming so overwhelmed with different emotions. He doesn't really know what to think of his mother. Nia begins to cry as well. "Javier, I am so sorry please forgive me, please!" Javier asks, "why did you stay away?" "You never came to any of the barbeques your own family had." "It was because I was too afraid to face you son." "Please don't think any of this was easy for me." "I've thought of you so much over the years." "My mistake of leaving you behind has haunted me up until this day." "If you give me the chance to enter into your life, I promise to be the best mom I can be." "I do forgive you." "This will take time for me to be comfortable and come around." "But everyday going forward I'm sure we can come closer to becoming a family that we should've been." Javier leans in and gives Nia a hug and she thanks him for the opportunity to move forward. She then introduces him to her fiancé as they all sit down and embrace each other.

Over the next few days Javier and Nia became better acquainted with one another. Filling in the blanks of the years of not being together, sharing photos of graduations and birthdays. "This is my graduation pictures from kindergarten," Javier explains. "This is me at Virginia Beach learning how to surf." "That was a great day for me." "Dolphins were swimming all around me, jumping in and out of the water." "That's why I like dolphins so much and they're also my best team in the NFL." Nia smiles and say, "you're such a handsome young man, I can't wait for us to begin creating our memories together son." She then offers her son to be a part of her upcoming wedding and he accepts the offer. "What would I do?" "I never been in a wedding before." "I don't know we will figure it out, we haven't made any official plans yet." She then opens her old notebook filled with poems she wrote as a little girl. "As a child I loved to write as I do today as a journalist." "This is a collection of poems I've written when I felt the urge to write." "I want you to have them as a token of my love." Javier accepts the gift. "In that book you will find a poem called "Choices," I want you to read it when you have the chance." "I've written that poem one day when I found out I was pregnant with you." "It doesn't talk about my pregnancy at all, but it is about choices, because we all have to make them on a daily basis." "Some of us will make the right choices depending on our circumstances and others will do what they believe or perceive to be right." "Some may consider everyone that is involved in the situation to the given circumstance." "Others will be selfish and make decisions based on their needs only." "However, each choice that we make will affect us in a positive or negative way." "Though I never been to jail, but I have been prisoned by my actions, haunted by my thoughts." Nia kisses Javier on the forehead and tells him she loves him. That day Nia decides to move back to central Virginia to be closer to her first-born child as their relationship continues to grow. She also made a promise to never leave his side again. Over the years they had challenges but never strayed away from each other.

Song: *"The Choices We Make"*
Every day we wake up with a choice
To speak up or stay silent with our voice
To give love or to hold it all inside
To let go or to hold on tight
Sometimes it feels like we're lost in a maze
But we have the power to change our ways
Our destiny is in our hands
It's up to us to take a stand
The choices we make, shape our lives
They can bring us joy or cause us to strive
Every decision we make counts
It's up to us to choose the amount
We can take a risk or play it safe
We can follow the crowd or pave our own way
We can choose to be happy or let sadness reign
We can choose to heal or let pain remain
Sometimes it feels like we're stuck in a rut
But we have the power to break the shut
Our destiny is in our hands
It's up to us to make a stand
The choices we make, shape our lives
They can bring us joy or cause us to strive
Every decision we make counts
It's up to us to choose the amount
Life is a journey with twists and turns
We can learn and grow or let it burn
Our future is not set in stone
We can choose to rise or let it fall
The choices we make, shape our lives
They can bring us joy or cause us to strive
Every decision we make counts

It's up to us to choose the amount
The choices we make, the choices we make
Every decision counts, it's never too late.

Don't miss out!

Visit the website below and you can sign up to receive emails whenever Daryl Young publishes a new book. There's no charge and no obligation.

https://books2read.com/r/B-A-IUTX-GRTHC

BOOKS 2 READ

Connecting independent readers to independent writers.